written by Marcia Trimble • • illustrated by Susan Arciero

The Smiling Stone

Images Press – Los Altos Hills, California

Text copyright © 1998 by Marcia Trimble
Illustration copyright © 1998 by Susan Arciero

Publisher's Cataloging-in-Publication
(Provided by Quality Books, Inc.)

Trimble, Marcia.
     The Smiling Stone / by Marcia Trimble; illustrated by Susan Arciero. – 1st ed.
     p.   cm.
     Preassigned LCCN: 98-92502
     ISBN: 1-891577-37-9
     Summary: Smiling all the way, a small stone makes a journey from a Nantucket Beach
on the Atlantic Ocean to a little pond.
     [1. Pebbles–Juvenile poetry. 2. Voyages and travels–Juvenile poetry. 3. Smile–Juvenile
poetry.]   I. Arciero, Susan.   II. Title.

PZ8.3.T75 1998   811'.54 [E]
QBI98-121

10 9 8 7 6 5 4 3 2 1

Text was set in Comic Sans MS
Book design by MontiGraphics

Printed in Hong Kong by South China Printing Co. (1988) Ltd. on acid free paper. ∞

For Malinda, the smile of my life. M.T.

For Jake, who brings a smile into my studio everyday. S.A.

A   wee

tiny stone...

lies on the beach...

smiling up at the sun...

smiles till the day is done.

A wee tiny stone
lies on the path

smiling at a passerby...

smiles a great big "hi".

A wee tiny stone
lies under a branch

smiling up at the tree...

smiles up at Timothy.

A wee tiny stone
flies by the pond...

smiling up at the bird...
smiles as if chirping a word.

A wee tiny stone
lies in the garden
smiling up at the rose...
smiles from its head
to its toes.

A wee tiny stone
lies by the doghouse
smiling up at the dog...

smiles right through
the morning fog.

A wee tiny stone
lies by the gate
smiling up at the cat...
smiles at the child
giving a pat.

The child giving the pat
looks at the wee tiny stone...

smiles a smile of her own
and tips her hat.

A smile on your face
is yours to give

smiles
the wee tiny stone.

Your smile casts forever a beam of light.

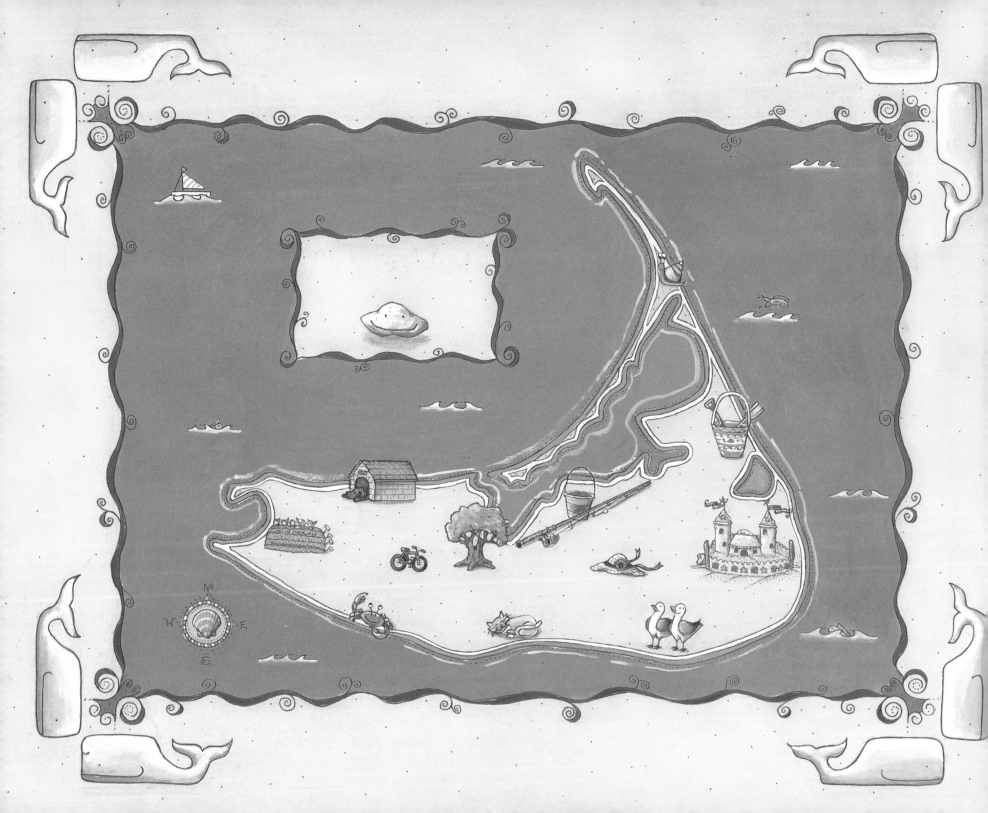